Christmas in the Trenches

Elizabeth Shields

Reading Level

Age / Interest Level: 12+
Lexile Level: 770L
Grade Level Equivalent: 3.6

ISBN: 978-1-64261-5-050

Cover design by Story Shares

www.storysharescontest.org

Printed in the United States of America

Boston. New York. Philadelphia.

Chapter 1

Thomas

December 24, 1914

World War I

The British Trenches of the Western Front

I could not remember being colder than I was that night. It could have been the weather. Or maybe it was the general feeling in the air. Huddling together under hand-made shelters, we knew what the others were thinking without having to ask.

This was our first Christmas in the trenches. How many holidays would we spend here? How many more would we live to see? I closed my eyes, thinking of the tree my family was decorating without me. And there were carol services I would not attend for the first time in twenty years. And my younger sister asking my mother if Saint Nicholas would still come in times of war.

The fallen snow had been pressed into mud in the bottom of each trench. Oh, how I wanted a shining winter view like those in Yorkshire! I saw no Christmas trees here. I heard no carols—only the coughing of some poor bloke who could hardly breathe between his fits. There were no Christmas delights. There were only the harsh rations I'd gotten used over these months.

"You'd better get some sleep, Thomas," someone said to me. "I doubt the Germans will be letting you take Christmas off."

It was true, but I didn't think I'd get much rest tonight. I moved under a shelter and pulled my coat tight, trying to remember what it meant to be warm. Then I noticed soft voices coming from the German trenches.

"*O kommet, o kommet nach Bethlehem!*"

It was to the tune of "Oh Come, All Ye Faithful," and I suppose that's what it was.

"As if the Germans are faithful. As if they deserve to see the Christ." A nearby man spat at the ground and lit a cigar. I smiled as a second man told him something. I'd rather not repeat it, but it summed up my feelings.

I had not thought I'd get any sleep, but I found myself dozing off to the rich, German voices filling the air with their carols. It was no English carol service, but it was close enough for me.

.

Chapter 2

Heinrich

December 25, 1914

World War I

The German Trenches of the Western Front

"Leuchten meine zigarre, ja?" Kurt held out the mostly burnt stump to me. I did as he asked and watched him smile as he slowly puffed smoke into the icy air. There was nothing better to do than watch the smoke curl up into the grey sky.

"God in heaven, perhaps you would make this Christmas be without gunfire," Kurt said between puffs.

"Amen," I said, leaning against the side of the trench.

There was a sound from around the trenches. The watchmen shouted. For a minute, we thought our prayer had been rejected. We drew our guns when a British soldier stepped out of the enemy trenches. I climbed a ladder, pointing my own gun toward him, whatever he may be doing.

But his hands were raised.

Slowly, our captain climbed out. We watched with surprise as the two men walked toward each other. They covered hundreds of yards, through barbed wire. They met halfway and stood for a moment. Then they shook hands, sharing words we tried, but were unable, to hear. Fear and mistrust spread through the trenches.

"Happy Christmas!" the British man shouted, loud enough for all the world to hear. Our fear became surprise. Slowly, more British troops climbed from their trenches.

We began to climb out, too. We felt unsure as we took those steps. But nobody from the British side was armed. It wasn't a trick. It was simply Christmas.

We walked after our leaders, through the barbed wire and over the frozen ground. Our lines met. As we came together, we stared at the other unit. Nobody was quite sure what to do. But those in front began wishing the others a "*Frohe Weihnacht*"—a Merry Christmas—shaking hands and holding out simple gifts. The language barrier was still present but had faded in all the holiday cheer.

A man around my age walked up to me and held out an English cigar. Smiling, he pressed it into my hand.

"*Danke,*" I said, figuring he would understand I was saying thank you. He nodded.

"My name is Thomas," he said.

"*Mein name ist Heinrich,*" I replied, fairly sure I was understanding him. We shook hands. I dug through my pockets to find an unused cigar of my own. Thomas smiled when I gave it to him.

Someone waved a ball in the air to begin a game of football. It fell to the Germans versus the British. I am glad to say we won. But kicking the ball around and shooting goals past the British goalie—well, it made me forget the sides.

Thomas tried to teach me a card game. I had no idea what he was saying. After a while we gave up. A little later, everyone sang carols together, in their different languages: "*Stille Nacht*" mixed with "Silent Night." The German and British voices mixed under the sky. On that day, the stars seemed to have no conflict beneath them.

But it would be anything but a *stille nacht*. Distant sounds of guns and artillery stopped our singing. And we knew it was over.

Everyone ran back to their own trenches, leaving their cigars and playing cards with their enemies. Others smoked them and played with them, but not me. I wanted to save that cigar as a reminder that every Christmas will have gifts and joy, even if it seems impossible.

We were back to fighting the next day, killing men that for a day had been our comrades. Maybe next Christmas, we would again get along for twenty four hours. We all thought it wouldn't happen to begin with. But after all, we'd had a Christmas in the trenches.

Chapter 3

Christmas Once Again

December 25, 1916

World War I

A veteran's hospital in England

It felt like the first time I had smiled in two years. Lying in bed, unable to move half of my body, I was happier than I had been in a long time. There were cookies and a Christmas card next to my bed. My little sister had put them there. She no longer believed in Saint Nicholas. I was the only one in the family who still had faith in Christmas miracles.

The man in the bed next to me stirred, and a nurse came over. "What day is it?" he asked.

"Christmas," the nurse replied. His face lit up.

I sighed. My holiday would be much better spent than too many men. The Christmas peace two years ago seemed a lifetime away. Last year, my unit, along with many others, failed to honor Christ's birth. This year, we'd received word that it wouldn't happen at all.

It hardly mattered. The men we'd been friends with had been blown away the next day. My German friend, Heinrich, had died December 27. I'd nearly stepped on his body running back to my home trenches. I never lit the German made cigar he'd given me. It was the only Christmas present I'd received in 1914.

Several times in combat I had nearly lost it. Now it stayed in my jacket pocket, next to my bed. I pulled it out, twisting the limp paper in my hand several times. Despite all it had been through, it still looked usable.

The nurse hummed a Christmas carol. It took a moment to know it before I began to hum along. Soon I was singing quietly, but the words were not in English.

"*O kommet, o kommet nach Bethlehem!*"

The man in the next bed looked over at me.

"You were there?"

I nodded.

"So was I." He paused for a few seconds. "You know, there's a lot about this war that I won't be able forget. I think that's the only part I'll remember for being good."

"It was a day we were all men, not just soldiers."

He joined me for the last refrain.

"*O lasset uns anbeten,*

O lasset uns anbeten, O lasset uns anbeten

Den König, den Herrn!"

The nurse gave us a strange look before walking away.

"What's your name?" I asked the man.

"Henry Fisher," he replied.

"Henry," I said. "Would you like a cigar?"

Story Shares is a nonprofit focused on supporting the millions of teens and adults who struggle with reading by creating a new shelf in the library specifically for them. The growing collection features content that is compelling and culturally relevant for teens and adults, yet still readable at a range of lower reading levels.

Story Shares generates content by engaging deeply with writers, bringing together a community to create this new kind of book. With more intriguing and approachable stories to choose from, the teens and adults who have fallen behind are improving their skills and beginning to discover the joy of reading. For more information, visit storysharescontest.org.

Easy to Read. Hard to Put Down.

Notes:

Notes:

Notes:

Notes:

13

Notes:

Notes:

Notes:

Notes:

Notes:

Notes:

Notes:

Notes:

Notes:

Made in United States
North Haven, CT
07 June 2022

19966112R00017

Story Shares

There are no Christmas trees, no carols,
no holiday delights, and yet...
the spirit of Christmas remains alive
in the most unlikely of circumstances.

Relevant Reads

Easy to Read. Hard to Put Down.

Christmas In The Trenches | Elizabeth Shields
Fiction

ISBN 9781642615050

90000

9 781642 615050

Earth's
Shipping
Yard

Todd
Rykaczewski